my many emotions

Anger

Cherry Lake Press

Published in the United States of America by Cherry Lake Publishing Group
Ann Arbor, Michigan
www.cherrylakepublishing.com

Reading Adviser: Beth Walker Gambro, MS, Ed., Reading Consultant, Yorkville, IL
Content Adviser: Emily Fragapane, M.Ed., Ed.S., Nationally Certified School Psychologist, RYT200
Book Designer: Jennifer Wahi
Illustrator: Jeff Bane

Photo Credits: © Jamie Katherine Peacock/Shutterstock.com, 5; © Prostock-studio/Shutterstock.com, 7; © Joaquin Corbalan P/Shutterstock.com, 9; © Suzanne Tucker/Shutterstock.com, 11; © Tom Wang/Shutterstock.com, 13; © antoniodiaz/Shutterstock.com, 15; © Eakachai Leesin/Shutterstock.com, 17; © pixelheadphoto digitalskillet/Shutterstock.com, 19; © Chutima Chaochaiya/Shutterstock.com, 21; © granata68/Shutterstock.com, 23; Cover, 2-3, 6, 14, 22, 24, Jeff Bane

Cherry Lake Press is an imprint of Cherry Lake Publishing Group.

Library of Congress Cataloging-in-Publication Data

Names: Devera, Czeena, author. | Bane, Jeff, 1957- illustrator.
Title: Anger / by Czeena Devera ; illustrated by Jeff Bane.
Description: Ann Arbor, Michigan : Cherry Lake Publishing, [2022] | Series: My many emotions | Includes index. | Audience: Grades K-1
Identifiers: LCCN 2021004891 (print) | LCCN 2021004892 (ebook) | ISBN 9781534186934 (hardcover) | ISBN 9781534188334 (paperback) | ISBN 9781534189737 (pdf) | ISBN 9781534191136 (ebook)
Subjects: LCSH: Anger--Juvenile literature. | Emotional intelligence--Juvenile literature. | Social learning--Juvenile literature.
Classification: LCC BF575.A5 D48 2022 (print) | LCC BF575.A5 (ebook) | DDC 152.4/7--dc23
LC record available at https://lccn.loc.gov/2021004891
LC ebook record available at https://lccn.loc.gov/2021004892

Printed in the United States of America
Corporate Graphics

table of contents

About the author: Czeena Devera grew up in the red-hot heat of Arizona surrounded by books. Her childhood bedroom had built-in bookshelves that were always full. She now lives in Michigan with an even bigger library of books.

About the illustrator: Jeff Bane and his two business partners own a studio along the American River in Folsom, California, home of the 1849 Gold Rush. When Jeff's not sketching or illustrating for clients, he's either swimming or kayaking in the river to relax.

Have you ever felt something bubble up inside you? Something you may feel like you can't contain? That's **Anger**.

How would you describe Anger?

Anger can be quiet or loud. It can last a long or short while.

Anger can come when things feel **unfair**. Maybe you want to play with your friends, but you can't. This can be hard.

Sometimes, other feelings can lead to Anger. You might be **frustrated** with homework. Or you might be sad about losing a game.

You might feel Anger when someone hurts your feelings.

How does Anger feel to you?

You might get a headache. Or your tummy might not feel so well. Your face may feel hot. Your thoughts might feel like they're racing.

You might want to throw something. Or shout. Or cry. These are all normal **reactions**. Anger should be **expressed** and not bottled up.

But expressing feelings shouldn’t hurt others or yourself. Take time to slow down. Write down how you’re feeling. Talk to a trusted adult.

Focus on your breathing. Breathe in. Breathe out. Make a fist with your hand. Ball it up really tight. Then, let it go.

How do you show Anger?

Remember, it's okay to feel Anger. It comes and goes. It doesn't last forever.

glossary & index

glossary

anger (AN-guhr) a strong feeling of displeasure or annoyance

expressed (ek-SPRESSED) showed feelings or thoughts by saying, doing, or writing something

frustrated (FRUHSS-tray-uhd) discouraged or upset because of being unable to do or complete something

reactions (ree-AK-shuhns) behaviors or responses to something

unfair (uhn-FAYR) not fair, honest, or just

index